The Winter of the Little Brown Bat

by Elise Smith
illustrated by Lisa Desimini

MODERN CURRICULUM PRESS
Pearson Learning Group

Meet the little brown bat.
It weighs less than half an ounce!
Its wingspan is between nine and
eleven inches. The little brown bat
is widespread in North America. It is
the most common bat in the United
States and Canada.

The little brown bat lives in almost
any environment where there are many
kinds of insects—woods, lakes, and
ponds. Sometimes, at night, you can see
this bat against the glow of a street lamp.
The little brown bat is nocturnal. This
means it sleeps during the day and is active
at night.

The bat is a mammal. It is the only mammal that flies. The bat is also a predator. In spring and summer, the little brown bat eats many insects. It hunts by streams and marshes. It eats mosquitoes, moths, gnats, grasshoppers, and other flying insects. The little brown bat can eat hundreds of insects in a single day!

The little brown bat does not immediately use all the energy those insects provide. It stores some energy as fat. During the long, cold months of winter, there are not many insects to eat. There is not enough food for the bat. But it does not starve during those frosty days and nights. Its body changes the stored fat into energy. It does this during hibernation.

What is hibernation? Hibernation is like a deep sleep. Hibernation allows animals such as chipmunks, hamsters, and the little brown bat to live through a long, cold winter. If the weather is cold enough, the bat might start to hibernate as early as September. If the weather stays cold, it might continue to hibernate until May!

During spring and summer, the little brown bat stores more and more energy as fat. When it goes into hibernation, it chooses a sheltered place. Its breathing slows down. Its heart rate drops from about nine hundred beats per minute to about twenty beats per minute. Its body temperature lowers.

SUMMER
Bat stores fat.

SPRING
Bat begins to store
fat from food it eats.

WINTER
Bat hibernates.

8

During hibernation the bat uses very little energy. It survives the long winter by using all the energy it stored during the warm weather. Heat is produced by the fat as it burns. The heat moves through the little brown bat's blood. It keeps the muscles in shape during the months when the bat is not active.

FALL
Bat may begin
to hibernate.

During hibernation, the bat might roost in an old spindly tree, an abandoned building, or the attic of a house. Sometimes, it roosts in an old stone chimney or a cave. The bat holds on with toe claws. Many bats hang close together. The body heat produced by the group provides extra warmth for each bat.

The life of a hibernating little brown bat is fragile. If the temperature drops too low, a bat may die in its sleep. Sometimes, a bat wastes energy by flying away from people who wake it from its sleep. Then the bat might not have enough energy to survive the winter. It may die before spring comes. If the bat does survive, it can live to be thirty years old!

While hiking with your family or friends, you might come across fragile, hibernating bats. Do not shine a light on them. Do not touch them or make loud noises. We must respect the bats and their environment. Remember, the little brown bat helps us. It eats pesky, biting bugs!

If the little brown bat is left alone, it wakes up as the weather warms. Its body temperature rises. Its heart speeds up. It begins to breathe more rapidly. Finally, the bat wakes from hibernation. It is very hungry and ready to hunt for more insects!

There is a widespread fear of bats. Some people don't understand that many bats are extremely helpful to people. Bats eat many types of insects that destroy farmers' crops and our forests. Some bats help spread seeds that grow into useful plants. Others produce useful fertilizer to help grow crops. So the next time you see a bat, stop and think of all the things it can do to help people.